# The Ferryland Visitor
## A mysterious tale

by Charis Cotter

with artwork by Gerald L. Squires

They moved into the lighthouse in October.

"The spooky month," said Esther.

"The stormy month," said her father, looking out past the lighthouse to the wild blue Atlantic sea.

"The lonely month," said her sister Meranda.

"The cold month," said her mother, looking at the torn wallpaper flapping in the draft from the broken window.

No one had lived in the lighthouse keeper's house for seven years. The keepers and their families moved away when the lighthouse was automated. Now a man came out to check on it every few weeks, but gone were the days when the light had to be tended every day to make sure it never went out.

For seven years the house stood empty at the end of the narrow strip of land, beaten and battered by the wind and the sea. The windows were broken. The roof leaked. The house smelled of damp. No one had laughed or cried or shouted or slept in it for a long, long time.

Then Esther and her family moved in. It seemed the ideal place for her father to paint and her mother to make pots, with the wild, rocky shoreline for inspiration. Esther, who was six, and Meranda, who was seven, went to the local school in Ferryland, a two-mile walk along the road that wound from the lighthouse to the shore. They always knew when somebody was coming to visit, because they could see most of the road from the kitchen window—curving through the downs, inching along the narrows, twisting up the hill and disappearing around the corner.

Nobody came those first couple of weeks. Esther's parents were busy hammering up loose clapboard and replacing windows. Every day after school, Esther and Meranda explored the house and the rocks and the paths along the downs. The fall weather seemed to change every few minutes, from bright blue clear skies to cloudy grey ones; fog and rain blew in from the ocean and then blew out again.

The last week of October, just before Halloween, Esther was running along the path past the lighthouse, the sun on her face. The ocean was a deep, cobalt blue, stretching out on three sides of the point, stretching out forever. She stopped, lifted her arms and spun in a slow circle, taking in the ocean, the lighthouse, the headlands, the road to the shore— then dropped her arms and peered into the distance. Something was moving along the road, heading towards the lighthouse.

A string of animals? Esther put up her hand to shade her eyes. Sheep? No, too big. Cows? She couldn't tell.

She jumped over a rock, ran down the hill and set off along the road to meet them. As they got closer, she could see they weren't cows at all, but horses. At least a dozen brown and black horses.

"What're you looking at, Esther?" called her father. He was down at the well, filling up the water buckets. There was no running water in the lighthouse, so they had to fetch all their water from the well.

"Horses!" said Esther. "Coming down the road."

He looked up. The horses were crossing the narrows now, in single file. Behind them a cloud of fog drifted down from the hill.

Esther's dad lay the carrying hoop across the buckets and, stepping inside it, picked them up by the handles. The hoop kept the buckets balanced and cut down on the water sloshing over the edge as he walked. He headed back towards the lighthouse, Esther skipping along beside him.

"Where do the horses come from?" she asked.

"Ferryland. When the weather's good, their owners let them roam wherever they want to."

"That's what I'd like best if I was a horse," said Esther, balancing on a small rock for a few seconds and then jumping off. "Running free, wherever I want to go."

Her father smiled. "Wait till next summer. When school's over you can run around free like a Newfoundland pony all summer."

The horses caught up with them and slowly passed, tails flicking. For a few minutes Esther and her father were in the middle of the herd. Then the horses moved on ahead. The fog came right along behind them, swirling around their feet and creeping up over the bushes at the side of the road. Esther looked back. She couldn't see the far side of the narrows any more.

"You know why they come?" said her father, picking his way carefully on the rocky road. "Arch told me the horses always come out to the lighthouse when there's fog rolling in. The fog makes the grass taste sweeter. So if you see the horses coming along the road, you know we're in for some weather."

Esther plucked a long piece of grass from the side of the road and nibbled on the root end.

"Yes," she said. "I think they're right. Very sweet."

Her father laughed and they went on up the hill to the lighthouse.

Esther went into the kitchen where her mother, Meranda, and Houndie, their dog, were building a wooden bench. Meranda was handing nails to her mum, who was hammering away. Houndie watched, her head on her paws.

"Where have you been?" said her mum. "The fog's rolling in."

Esther looked out the window. A greyish white cloud was drifting up from the south, obscuring parts of the shore and the road. To the north she could see the dim shapes of the horses grazing on the downs. She sat down by the window and watched clumps of grass and rocks disappear and then appear again as the fog crept along the headland.

Behind her she could hear her mother and sister hammering and talking. Then her father came in. Their voices faded away and she got that strange, fainty feeling she'd been having a lot lately. She leaned her head on the cold new glass of the window. The fog had lifted a bit now and she could see the road all the way to the narrows.

Suddenly there was a knock at the door. Esther jumped.

"Who on earth?" said her mother.

Esther followed her father into the hallway. A tall man was standing just inside the front door. Houndie sat at his feet, thumping her tail and looking up at the visitor with a big dog smile on her face. That was strange. Houndie took her role as a watchdog very seriously and always barked her head off any time anyone came near their old house. But this time she hadn't made a peep.

"Good day, sir." The stranger had a creaky voice. "Your dog asked me to come in."

From what Esther could see in the dark hallway, the man was wearing a long black coat that brushed the top of his big boots. Around his neck was a white collar.

Esther had seen those white collars before. This must be the local priest, she thought, come to welcome us to Ferryland. She took a step closer.

Esther's father laughed.

"Well then, you had better come in," he said. "Houndie is a very serious dog and it's best to do what she says."

The big man came forward, handing his coat to Esther's father. Then she saw he wasn't a priest at all, just a man wearing a white turtleneck sweater. He lumbered into the kitchen, greeted the others and sat down in the chair closest to the glowing woodstove. The few strands of hair left on his mostly bald head were white, and his face grizzly with wrinkles.

He seemed a bit stiff, from the cold, perhaps. Esther's mother offered him a cup of tea and soon they were all sitting around the kitchen table having a chat.

The man told them he'd come by to see what the new people in the lighthouse were like.

"I've been coming out to this lighthouse for a long time," he said, smiling at Esther. "I was good friends with the last keeper, and I've spent many a night out here with him, watching the TV. He had it before anyone else along here, because he had the electricity and we didn't."

The man went on to tell them he used to be Ferryland's policeman. Esther's mother and father asked him questions about the old days, and the man spun a tale or two. He told them about a boy who had caught pneumonia and died in the lighthouse, and showed them where the body was laid out for the wake. After a few more cups of tea, and a drink of whisky, he told them about the many other wakes he'd attended at the lighthouse, the storms he'd seen, the people who had come and gone.

He twinkled his eyes at Esther and after a while she went and sat on his lap to listen to his stories. He smelled like tobacco. At one point he fished in his jacket pocket and came up with a quarter to give her. Esther held it tightly. That was a lot of money; she could buy two chocolate bars and some bubblegum with it the next time they went to the store.

After his second glass of whisky, he started telling Bible stories, but they seemed a bit mixed up. He had Jacob swallowed by a whale instead of Jonah, and Abraham parting the Red Sea instead of Moses. Esther knew better than that, but everyone was having fun and no one corrected him.

Finally he stood up to go.

"Thank you for your hospitality. I'm happy to meet you all, and now I know you'll be good for this lighthouse. It's still the friendly spot it always was." He leaned over and patted Houndie on the head. "Goodbye, old fella."

Esther's dad walked him out. After the door closed behind him, Esther's mum stood up and began to clear the table. Esther drifted over to her spot by the window and examined her quarter in the light. It was a bit grimy, so she gave it a rub with the end of her t-shirt. She could just make out the date: 1950. She looked up and along the road. Streamers of fog still hung along the shore, but she could see way past the narrows. The road was empty.

Her mother came up behind her and put her hands on Esther's shoulders, peering out.

"Where'd he get to?" she asked. "Did he just fly away?"

"Maybe's he's taking a look around," said Esther's dad, loading some logs into the woodstove.

"I didn't see him arrive, either," said her mother. Then she turned back into the kitchen to clear the cups and saucers off the table.

Esther sat down in the chair by the window. "Neither did I," she whispered. She had that fainty feeling again, and took some deep breaths. Behind her the family was busy with this and that, but Esther didn't move. She could see the horses, still up on the downs. The fog was nearly gone now, and the road was clear as far as the turn on the hill.

A long time later her mother came up behind her again.

"Any sign of our visitor, Esther?"

"Nope."

"That's strange," said her mother.

The next day Esther drove with her father to visit Arch, a friend who lived on the other side of the hill. Her dad and Arch talked about how they were settling in, what repairs they were doing to the lighthouse.

Aunt William's House

"Oh, and we had our first visitor yesterday," said Esther's dad. "A very friendly guy, an old timer."

"Who was that?" asked Arch. "I didn't see anyone go past."

"Well, we never did get his name, did we Esther?"

She shook her head.

"But he said he used to be a policeman in Ferryland, and he was good friends with the lighthouse keeper in the old days. He told us lots of stories about the lighthouse, one about a little boy who died of pneumonia out there, after falling into the water in cold weather."

"Hmmm," said Arch. "A policeman, you say?"

"Yes, a constable."

"What did he look like?" asked Arch.

"Tall, nearly bald, long black coat. Big mouth, blue eyes, long nose."

"Sticky-out ears," added Esther. "And he gave me a quarter."

"Lucky you," said Arch. "Look, Gerry, I don't want to alarm you but the man you describe, and that story about the little boy, well, it sounds like Dick Costello. I don't know who else it could be. He was the constable around here for many years, and that boy dying, that happened in his time. And he was good friends with the keeper, out there a few nights every week, just for the company."

"Yes, that's what he said. He said he used to watch TV there, before anyone else had it."

Arch nodded his head. "That's true, but here's the odd thing." He paused and gave Esther's dad a strange look.

"Yes? What's the odd thing?"

Arch glanced at Esther and then back to her dad. "Well, it couldn't have been Dick Costello. He died twenty years ago."

Esther felt the fainty feeling stronger than ever and clutched at her father's arm.

"What?" said her father, starting to laugh. "You're kidding me, right, Arch?"

Arch shook his head.

"No. He's dead all right. And yet the man you described is the spitting image of him."

As the cold winter wore on, Esther and her family slowly adapted to life in the lighthouse. They ate, slept, and worked in the kitchen because the rest of the house was too cold. The "lighthouse girls," as they were called by the kids at school, had to walk with their dad all the way to school on the days when the ice made it impossible to drive the windy road along the narrows and over the hill. The winter seemed very long.

Spring came, finally. And that summer Esther ran free like a Newfoundland pony, just as her father had said she would. She went out in the morning and wasn't seen again until lunch, playing on the rocks and exploring the downs. And every time she saw a string of horses making their way across the narrows, she looked up to see if the fog was rolling in. It always was.

Her mother opened a pottery shop in the lighthouse and sunny days brought lots of visitors. One day, Esther was wrapping up a piece of pottery for a customer while her father counted out her change. Esther noticed that he kept giving the woman funny looks, as if he wanted to ask her something. She was a tall woman, with a squarish face, and something about her was familiar.

"You sound like you're from the States," said Esther's dad.

"Yes," said the woman. "You wouldn't know I was born right around here, from the way I talk, now would you?"

She told them she'd grown up near Ferryland but had married an American and moved away years before.

"I guess I lost my Newfoundland accent after all those years away. I have family here, and I finally came back for a visit," she said.

"I'm going to make a guess," said Esther's dad. "You're Dick Costello's daughter."

Esther edged over to her dad and took a hold of his sleeve, tight.

Now it was the woman's turn to stare.

"How did you know that?" she said.

"You look just like him," said Esther's dad. "I knew there was something familiar about you the minute you walked in the shop. I couldn't place it till now."

"When did you meet my dad?" asked the woman. "You're not from here."

"Well," said Esther's father slowly, "I think we had a visit from him last fall."

He took the astonished woman by the arm and led her outside to sit on a bench in the sun, Esther trailing along behind. Then he told her the whole story, from the knock at the door until the time the man walked out the door, never to be seen again. As she listened, the look of wonder on her face grew. She kept shaking her head and making startled little noises.

"I've never heard anything like this," she said when the story was over. "It certainly sounds like my dad. He told me many of those same stories when I was growing up. He loved this lighthouse. It was like his second home." Her eyes glistened with tears.

"The most amazing thing is what he said when you first saw him. That's what convinces me it really was my dad."

"What's that?" said Esther's dad.

"Well, Dad was known around here to always say the same thing when he walked into someone's house. He visited a lot of people: that was part of his job. He'd knock at the door and then walk right in and say exactly the same thing every time."

The woman started to laugh, tears still trickling down her face.

"What did he say?" asked Esther.

The woman looked down at her.

"He'd say, "Your dog asked me to come in.""

## AUTHOR'S NOTE

This is a true story: it happened in the 1970s when artist Gerry Squires moved with his family into the lighthouse keeper's house at Ferryland, Newfoundland. Esther and Gerry both told me their versions of the story.

Dick Costello was a constable in Ferryland who died in 1952. According to his grandson, Doug Grahn, Costello loved telling stories and had a lively sense of humour. Arch Williams, a good friend to the Squires, lived along the road to the shore.

I had many cups of tea with Esther, talking about her childhood in Ferryland. This book is a reflection of her memories of that magical time and place.

~

Thank you Esther, Gerry, Gail and Meranda for sharing your stories with me. And a big thank you to the Access Copyright Foundation for their support for this project.

~ Charis Cotter

access COPYRIGHT
FOUNDATION

33

## PUBLISHER'S NOTE

The story of the mysterious visitor to the Ferryland lighthouse is one I have long loved. I first heard Gerry and Gail Squires tell it in Stuart Pierson and Janet Kergoat's kitchen, not long after my family and I moved to Newfoundland. I've never forgotten the thrill of hearing it that evening. When Charis Cotter approached me about publishing her retelling of it, it seemed only natural to ask Gerry to provide the artwork.

We planned a beautiful, slightly spooky book for young readers. But, thanks to the cooperation and generosity of the entire Squires family, what we have is all that and much more—a celebration of a unique time in a very special family's life. Gerry Squires died of cancer before this book was finished; his death has been a profound loss for the Newfoundland and Labrador cultural community, and for those who knew and loved him. We were so happy to be able to share the next-to-last draft of the layout and design with Gerry before his illness took its last turn. Our deepest thanks to the Squires family for continuing to work with grace and great-heartedness on this project during such a difficult time; we hope it is some small contribution to the ongoing remembrance of a beautiful spirit and a life lived with great integrity, compassion and vision.

Thanks, too, to Doris (Costello) Grahn and her son Doug Grahn, for their enthusiastic support for this book, and their permission to use the photograph of Doris's father.

~ Marnie Parsons

## LIST OF IMAGES

### List of Paintings

Cover: "Coming on Duckish at Broad Cove",
2008 oil on canvas, 24"H x 30"W: photo by Ray Fennelly

p. 4:  "The Narrows on the Road to the Ferryland Lighthouse",
2013 oil on canvas, 36"H x 48"W: photo by Graham Blair

p. 8:  "The Gathering,"
2005 oil on canvas, 5'H x 7'W: photo by John Haney

p. 12: "Hare Ears Island, South End,"
2006 oil on canvas, 20"H x 24"W: photo by Ray Fennelly

p. 19: "Mystic Cloud,"
2005 oil on canvas, 36"H x 40"W: photo by Ray Fennelly

p. 23: detail, "Ferryland Lighthouse,"
1986  oil on canvas, 20" H x 28" W: photo by Esther Squires

p. 27: detail, "Dark Cave Under the Light,"
2006 oil on canvas, 20"H x 28"W: photo by Gail Squires

### List of Graphite Sketches

p. 3:   Southern Shore Headland and Islands

p. 6:   Ferryland Lighthouse

p. 11:  Newfoundland ponies

p. 20: Arch Williams' house

p. 24: Shoreline looking north

p. 28: Ferryland Light

p. 31: Bois Island, Ferryland

p. 36: Girl with water buckets

### Photographs

Photograph on p. 17 credited to Lynda Hendrickson; photograph on p. 33 used with the permission of Doug Grahn; photo on p. 34 credited to Martin Lyon; photographs on pages 13, 26, and the photo of Esther with kittens on p. 32 credited to Mannie Buchheit; all other photos credited to the Squires family. Every reasonable effort has been made to confirm the origin of photographs included in the book, and to obtain permission for their use; the publisher would be grateful for any information leading to correction of any oversight in this matter.

The typeface is Georgia, designed by Matthew Carter and inspired by the 19th-century
Scotch Roman typefaces. The book was designed by Veselina Tomova of Vis-à-Vis Graphics,
St. John's, Newfoundland and Labrador.

Printed in Canada.

We acknowledge the Canada Council for the Arts
for its financial support of our trade publishing program.

ISBN 978-1-927917-05-3

Running the Goat Books & Broadsides
50 Cove Road, Tors Cove, NL  A0A 4A0
www.runningthegoat.com